## Books by Sigmund Brouwer

**Lightning on Ice Series**
#1  *Rebel Glory*
#2  *All-Star Pride*
#3  *Thunderbird Spirit*
#4  *Winter Hawk Star*
#5  *Blazer Drive*
#6  *Chief Honor*

**Short Cuts Series**
#1  *Snowboarding to the Extreme . . . Rippin'*
#2  *Mountain Biking to the Extreme . . . Cliff Dive*
#3  *Skydiving to the Extreme . . . 'Chute Roll*
#4  *Scuba Diving to the Extreme . . . Off the Wall*

**CyberQuest Series**
#1  *Pharaoh's Tomb*
#2  *Knight's Honor*
#3  *Pirate's Cross* (available 8/97)
#4  *Outlaw Gold* (available 10/97)

**The Accidental Detectives Mystery Series**

**Winds of Light Medieval Adventures**

**Adult Books**
*Double Helix*
*Blood Ties*

# QUEST 1
# PHARAOH'S TOMB

## SIGMUND BROUWER

Thomas Nelson, Inc.
Nashville

**Pharaoh's Tomb**
Quest 1 in the *CyberQuest* Series

Published in Nashville, Tennessee,
by Tommy Nelson™, a division of Thomas Nelson, Inc.

Managing Editor: Laura Minchew
Project Editor: Beverly Phillips
Cover illustration: Kevin Burke

**Library of Congress Cataloging-in-Publication Data**

Brouwer, Sigmund, 1959–
    Pharaoh's tomb / Sigmund Brouwer.
        p. cm. — (CyberQuest ; #1)
    Summary: In a future world divided into the privileged
Technocrats and the poor Welfaros, Mok is taken from the slums
of Old Newyork by the Committee to be part of an experiment in
which the first test of his faith comes in ancient Egypt.
    ISBN 0-8499-4028-1
    [1. Science fiction.   2. Virtual reality—Fiction.
3. Christian life—Fiction.]   I. Title.   II. Series: Brouwer,
Sigmund, 1959–      CyberQuest ; #1.
PZ7.B79984Pj   1997
[Fic]—dc21                                              97-9999
                                                          CIP
                                                          AC

*Printed in the United States of America*
97 98 99 00 01 02 OPM 9 8 7 6 5 4 3 2 1

**To Michael and Jesse—**
**Thanks!**

# CYBERQUEST SERIES TERMS

**BODYWRAP** — a sheet of cloth that serves as clothing.

**THE COMMITTEE** — a group of people dedicated to making the world a better place.

**MAINSIDE** — any part of North America other than Old Newyork.

**MINI-VIDCAM** — a hidden video camera.

**NETPHONE** — a public telephone with a computer keypad. For a minimum charge, users can send e-mail through the Internet.

**OLD NEWYORK** — the bombed out island of Manhattan transformed into a colony for convicts and the poorest of the poor.

**TECHNOCRAT** — an upper class person who can read, operate computers, and make much more money than a Welfaro.

**'TRIC SHOOTER** — an electric gun that fires enough voltage to stun its target.

**VIDTRANS** — video transmitters.

**VIDWATCH** — a watch with a mini television screen.

**WATERMAN** — a person who sells pure water.

**WELFARO** — a person living in the slums in Old Newyork.

**THE GREAT WATER WARS—A.D. 2031.** *In the year*
*A.D. 2031 came the great Water Wars. The*
*world's population had tripled during the pre-*
*vious thirty years. Worldwide demand for fresh,*
*unpolluted water grew so strong that countries*
*fought for control of water supplies. The war*
*was longer and worse than any of the previous*
*world wars. When it ended, there was a new*
*world government, called the World United. The*
*government was set up to distribute water*
*among the world countries and to prevent any*
*future wars. But it took its control too far.*

*World United began to see itself as all-*
*important. After all, it had complete control of*
*the world's limited water supplies. It began to*
*make choices about who was "worthy" to re-*
*ceive water.*

*Very few people dared to object when World*
*United denied water to criminals, the poor, and*
*others it saw as undesirable. People were afraid*
*of losing their own water if they spoke up.*

*One group, however, saw that the govern-*
*ment's actions were wrong. These people dared*
*to speak—Christians.*

*They knew that only God should have control*

of their lives. They knew that they needed to stand up to the government for those who could not. Because of this, the government began to persecute the Christians and outlawed the Christian church. Some people gave up their beliefs to continue to receive an allotment of government water. Others refused and either joined underground churches or became hunted rebels, getting their water on the black market.

In North America, only one place was safe for the rebel Christians. The island of Old Newyork. The bombings of the great Water Wars had destroyed much of it, and the government used the entire island as a prison. The government did not care who else fled to the slums of those ancient street canyons.

Old Newyork grew in population. While most newcomers were criminals, some were these rebel Christians. Desperate for freedom, they entered this lion's den of lawlessness.

Limited water and supplies were sent from Mainside to Old Newyork, but some on Mainside said that any was too much to waste on the slums. When the issue came up at a World Senate meeting in 2049, it was decided that Old Newyork must be treated like a small country. It would have to provide something to the world in return for water and food.

When this new law went into effect, two things happened in the economy of this giant slum. First, work gangs began stripping steel from the skyscrapers. Anti-pollution laws on Mainside made it expensive to manufacture new steel. Old steel, then, was traded for food and water.

Second, when a certain Mainside business genius got caught evading taxes in 2053, he was sent to Old Newyork. There he quickly saw a new business opportunity—slave labor.

Old Newyork was run by criminals and had no laws. Who was there to stop him from forcing people to work for him?

Within a couple of years, the giant slum was filled with bosses who made men, women, and children work at almost no pay. They produced clothing on giant sewing machines and assembled cheap computer products. Even boys and girls as young as ten years old worked up to twelve hours a day.

Christians in Old Newyork, of course, fought against this. But it was a battle the Christians lost over the years. Criminals and factory bosses used ruthless violence to control the slums.

Christianity was forced to become an underground movement in the slums. Education, too, disappeared. As did any medical care.

Into this world, Mok was born.

# PROLOGUE

**MAINSIDE—A.D. 2076.** From the top of the cliff, giant searchlights slashed swords of white at the shoreline below. The black river released ghosts of fog that rose like gray smoke through the shafts of light. At the dock, where the ferries arrived and departed every four hours, soldiers patrolled the shoreline behind electric fences. Their dogs pulled them along by straining against their leashes.

Two men stood beneath the lights on the dock, waiting for the next ferry. They faced across the river. Searchlight circles danced across their backs, throwing flashes of long eerie shadows onto the water. The old man wore a long coat against the cold. A small suitcase rested near his feet. Standing beside him, a much younger man, shivered in a light jacket.

"Manhattan, Manhattan," the old man said. He coughed and spit red into a handkerchief. "Who would have thought it would come to this?"

"Manhattan?"

The older man smiled in apology. "Sorry," he said. "I was lost in thought. Before the great Water Wars, the island of Old Newyork was called Manhattan."

"Oh, yes," the younger man said. "I've seen photos on multimeed disks. Bridges once connected it to Mainside, right? Then the Water War bombs destroyed them."

"Bridges and tunnels." The old man pointed downriver. "A half mile away was the entrance to the tunnel called Lincoln. It went beneath the river and came up the other side on the island. In the gasoline era. They used it for automobiles."

"You remember that?"

The old man laughed at himself. "I *am* old, aren't I?"

He paused.

They both stared across the water. Each for different reasons. The older man had memories. The younger one had doubts.

The ghosts of fog were like shapeless soldiers, rising from the black deep. Past them, on the far shore, flickers of small fires appeared.

A coughing fit took the old man. It bent him almost to his waist.

The younger man waited until the other had regained his breath. Both pretended the coughing had not happened.

"There was once a time you could see the lights of Manhattan across the horizon," the old man said, searching for a way to break the awkward silence. "Lights of skyscrapers standing on the most expensive real estate in the world."

"And now," the young man said, "it's worse than worthless. A giant slum."

The young man needed to voice his earlier doubts. "Why should you offer them your help?"

As he spoke, a wide, flat-bottomed boat broke from the darkness into the spotlight circles. A bell rang on top of the hill. Within seconds, a dozen more spotlights burned through the night sky, bathing the ferry in a bright glare. The scene silenced both men on the dock.

In the boat's wake, three heads bobbed.

A sentry spotted the swimmers and blew a shrill whistle of warning. Soldiers shouted and dogs barked as all of the patrols moved toward the shore. Two dozen soldiers and dogs were waiting as the three swimmers staggered out of the water to be roped and marched toward the dock. They were barely more than boys, soaked and shivering, skinny and limping.

Both men on the dock remained silent as they watched the soldiers approach. The ferry was secured against the dock. The soldiers marched the three boys past the men and held them at rifle point near the end of the dock.

A large truck backed to the dock. Workers jumped out, pushed a ramp up to the side of the ferry, and began to unload large crates. Then they loaded food supplies onto the ferry for its return trip.

"Those three will be put on the ferry and returned to Old Newyork," the younger man said. "And you'll go with them, Benjamin. Are you sure this is what you must do?"

"As you grow older," Benjamin Rufus said, "you grow less certain of what is the right course of action and rely more on God's grace. Pray for me."

"Why must you go?" the younger man said with some impatience. "They are criminals and steel scavengers. They are the enemy. Surely there are better places to—"

"Think of the Cross," the old man said quietly.

The young man bowed his head.

"Cambridge," the old man said gently after a few moments. "You are not afraid to face difficult questions. That has been as important to me as your faith and intelligence."

The old man coughed again. He wiped his mouth and shook away his pain. "Your strength will make you the leader of the Committee when I am gone. Use the resources wisely."

Workers carried off the last of the crates. The soldiers prodded the three swimmers onto the ferry and handcuffed them to its rails.

"I want you to continue what I began here. Give the children hope." Benjamin Rufus leaned over and picked up his suitcase in his left hand. With his right, he reached out to shake Cambridge's hand.

"I'll be fine," Benjamin said. "By the time the ferry reaches the other side, I'll be dressed to move among them. I can make a difference there. And my illness won't kill me too soon. I'm a stubborn man. I'll send reports as long as I can."

"For the last time, sir, let me go. Take your money and return to the hospital. More treatment will—"

"Delay my death a year or two? No, Cambridge. Besides, I'm the only one on the Committee who can travel among them. I've been there before."

"You've been in Old Newyork?" Cambridge could not hide his shock.

Benjamin smiled. A passing searchlight showed the tired lines on his face. "Now, as I leave, I feel safe in telling you something I've kept hidden, even from the Committee. I was once sent there."

He paused and smiled sadly. "And that, of course, is why I must return."

With those last words, Benjamin Rufus left Cambridge standing alone.

Long after the ferry had slipped back into the darkness, Cambridge remained on the dock, staring at the water.

The old man had once been sent there! Yet only criminals were ever sent to Old Newyork.

*And he knows he will die among them,* Cambridge thought. *Otherwise he wouldn't have told me his secret.*

Cambridge also knew that getting into Old Newyork was simple. But once there, it was almost impossible to escape.

# CHAPTER 1

**MAINSIDE—TWENTY YEARS LATER (A.D. 2096).** The twelve Committee members chose a Friday early in February of 2096 as the day to kidnap Mok. They scheduled his trip to begin shortly after noon. The field ops had reported it was Mok's daily habit to nap at that time. They would find him in a crumbled portion of the abandoned subway tunnel that ran beneath Broadway.

By 9:00 A.M. on that Friday in February, eleven of the Committee members were seated in a luxury high-rise. The Committee owned the building, which sat on the west side of the Hudson River. All eleven sipped on imported water as they safely watched a vidtrans monitor Mok's last three hours in Old Newyork.

The twelfth Committee member was missing. He said he had a bad flu. It was a lie.

Besides those twelve, two others knew Mok's destination. They were level-five field ops. Both were in far more danger than the Committee in the high-rise. The field ops were stuck in the center of Old Newyork. They were doing their best to keep their mini-vidcams on Mok.

Mok, of course, knew nothing of this.

**OLD NEWYORK.** The field ops, Miles Steward and Lee D'Amico, had been waiting in the building shadows for five minutes, watching Mok.

Just down the street, Mok stood at the edge of a small crowd around a waterman. Sunlight glinted diamonds through the flasks of water on a rack behind the waterman. No pretty diamonds, however, glinted from the ugly machine-guns the guards on each side of the waterman carried.

Mok did not move. He stood taller than most in the crowd around him. He might have been a big fifteen-year-old. Or smaller at age twenty. Mok probably didn't know his age either. No hospitals meant no birth certificates. And bad nutrition meant slow growth.

The only thing certain about Mok was that his face—framed by dark, curly hair—showed a mixed background, a mongrel nobility of high cheekbones and faintly Asian eyes.

"Heat bomb," Miles said to his younger partner.

Miles was the taller of the two. Height was all that distinguished him from Lee at the moment, as both were dressed in formless bodywraps. They were as filthy and ragged as any of the Welfaros who

3

passed them in the crowds. Their faces were lost in the unkempt beards they had grown for this assignment; not a single one of their Mainside friends would have recognized them.

"Huh?" Lee replied. The mini-vidcam in his sleeve was directed at Mok and the waterman. But Lee's attention was on a rat that nosed the pants cuff of an old man nearby on the cracked pavement.

"Hit 'em with a heat bomb," Miles said, half indignant his junior partner didn't hang on his every word. "I tell you, kid, we should nuke 'em. Zap! Fuse all these Welfaros and their cockroach hotels into a puddle of glass. No more smell. No more garbage. No more food riots. And best of all, more water for the rest of us. I'll bet Mainside could save a couple million gallons a day."

Miles scratched his side. The old clothes were itchy. Or maybe it was fleas. He hoped it was the clothes.

Lee hardly heard his partner. He had just watched the rat crawl up the old man's pants leg. Head, body, then tail of the rat disappeared.

"Miles?"

"Yeah?"

"I think that guy's dead."

"What guy?" Miles didn't like it when his younger partner ignored his great ideas.

Lee pointed. "That guy. See the bump moving up his pants leg? It's a rat."

"No big deal," Miles said. "This is Old Newyork."

Not that either needed a reminder. Every breath

they took filled their nostrils with the stench of sewage from the gutters. Up and down the street, as far as they could see, rickety shacks filled the street canyons. Some shacks were lost in the shadows of the taller buildings. Other shacks were warmed by the morning's sunlight.

Miles softened his tough-guy voice. He told himself to remember this was only Lee's second time across the river. "Look, kid, you'll get used to it. Welfaros live different from Technocrats."

"They die different too." Lee couldn't take his eyes off the rat crawling beneath the man's clothes.

"Don't get bleeding heart on me," Miles said. "At least we haven't cut off their water. And—"

He broke off. "Your vidcam better be getting this. Look!"

Mok had moved to the stands and grabbed a water flask. He shouted at the waterman, waving the flask. Then Mok threw the water flask high and hard toward a nearby shack.

The waterman's guards, filled with horror at the possibility of seeing the flask shatter, dove to catch it. In that brief moment, Mok plucked another water flask from the stand and dashed back into the crowd.

Before the guards could raise their machine guns, the crowd broke into a stream of shouting, panicking people. Through the confusion, the waterman stared at the fleeing figure of Mok as he ducked and weaved his getaway.

"Did your vidcam get that?" Miles asked.

"All of it," Lee said. "Do we follow?"

"Of course. But not in a hurry. That's why you brushed up against him to plant that velcrotrak a half hour ago."

Miles paused. He let his voice get tough again. "Earlier you wondered if this was right. How do you feel now that you've seen he's low enough to steal pure water?"

# CHAPTER 3

**AS THEY MOVED** through the throngs of Welfaros, Miles and Lee were forced to be careful about several things. First of all, they didn't dare smile. Their teeth—white, straight, complete—would have given them away as Technocrats. Welfaros had stained and rotted teeth because Old Newyork did not have dentists.

Miles was also careful not to let anyone see him check the vidwatch on his wrist. The street grid on the watchface showed a pulsing red dot, which gave Mok's location. It should be easy to track Mok's movement. But if a Welfaro discovered technostuff could be had for the taking, Miles and Lee would be mobbed and killed. Their 'tric shooters might save them from a dozen Welfaros, but not from hundreds. So each time he looked at the vidwatch, Miles pretended to scratch his arm as he pulled back the sleeve of his bodywrap.

Because of their need to be careful, it took them half an hour to finally catch up with Mok. They passed Welfaros cooking chunks of meat over oil drums filled with burning garbage. They once stopped to let a work gang drag a steel girder past them down the street. They kept their heads down as a ganglord passed them, surrounded by guards armed with swords.

Finally, Miles and Lee turned down a side street, guided by the velcrotrak stuck to Mok's bodywrap.

"Here?" Lee whispered when Miles stopped and frowned at the broken-down entrance of a tall building.

"Here. Inside."

"Do we go in?" Lee asked.

"Are you nuts?" Miles replied. "There are thirty levels. He could be anywhere." Nothing, not even the invisible watching eyes of the Committee, could get Miles to step inside an unfamiliar Welfaro building. You never knew when and where the steel support girders had been thieved.

"Yatt Hote," Lee said as he craned his head to look at the entrance arches. "What kind of name is that to put on a building?"

Miles sighed. Ten years ago, when he'd gone through the Academy, pre–Water War history was as required as Basic Computer Wiring. This new generation of agents knew nothing.

"Hyatt Hotel," Miles said.

"Hotel?"

"Before the Water Wars, Technocrats used to visit here."

"From Mainside?"

"Where else? No one's come back from Mars yet."

"I mean—"

"Shhh!" Miles adjusted his ear phone. "The velcrotrak's hit voice activation."

"Send it on to Mainside?"

"Of course."

8

Lee pushed a switch on the vidcam strapped to his forearm. They both listened. The words were also sent on to the Committee in the luxury high-rise on the other side of the Hudson River.

"Water?" a reedy, wavering voice asked Mok, somewhere in the thirty levels of building above the field ops.

"You need it, don't you?" Miles and Lee recognized Mok's voice. Low, calm, and unhurried. They had yet to hear him speak differently.

"But this is pure!" she said. "Where did you get the credits?"

"It doesn't matter," Mok told her. "This should last you a few days."

"But nobody gives away pure water." The reedy voice broke into sobs. "And nobody cares about old women close to death."

"I've got to go," Mok said. "Hide the water. Make it last. I don't know when I can be back again."

Several moments of silence. Then the woman's voice reached them again. Faintly, as if Mok had already stepped into a hallway.

"Why have you done this for me?" she asked. "I can't pay you back."

More silence. Had Mok moved down the hallway? Or was he returning to answer the woman's question?

"All right." Mok's voice came in clearly. "I'll tell you why. If you laugh, I'll leave."

"I won't laugh." The old woman's voice was a whisper. Mok must be right beside her.

9

"The Galilee Man. His father's house has many rooms. He went there to prepare a place for us."

"I won't laugh, boy. But I don't understand."

"He said his followers who give the little ones a cup of cold water will truly get their reward."

"The Galilee Man? Who is he? Where did you hear this?"

"From an audiobook. I memorized it before it was stolen from me."

"Audiobook? Where did you get an—"

"Hush. Sip on some water. This book had wonderful tales about the man who walked in Galilee. I want to believe they are true. But no one I've asked can tell me if Galilee is a place or a legend."

"I surely cannot," the old woman said. "An audiobook! To think—"

"I listened to it again and again while I had it. There was a man in this audiobook. He gathered twelve men to follow him. Some were fishermen and—"

Mok's voice stopped abruptly. "What is this?"

"Looks like a spider without legs," the woman said moments later.

Miles and Lee shot glances at each other.

"He's found the velcrotrak," Miles said.

A loud snap nearly pierced their ears.

"He's *stepped* on the velcrotrak," Lee said. "Now what do we do?"

"Not a problem." Miles grinned. "We'll be waiting for him when he gets to his hiding hole."

# CHAPTER 4

**MAINSIDE**. The Committee member who had called in sick was not at home. He was hundreds of miles south of Old Newyork.

He stepped into a private suite in the main office of the World United government, where a man waited for him. This man's face was stretched tight in the highly fashionable manner of reconstructive surgery. He was the president of the World United— the most powerful person among the billions who had survived the Water Wars.

The Committee member bowed as he entered the room. Then he lifted his arms as if he were about to fly.

The president waved a detecto-wand around the man's body, searching for weapons and recording devices. Usually an assistant would do this, but no one else must know the Committee member was here. The detecto-wand remained silent.

Finally satisfied, the president nodded to allow the other to speak.

"I am here to tell you that the Committee is ready to test another candidate, your Worldship."

"And?" the leader of the World United prompted. He wore the black silk toga that signified a high-status

Technocrat. He was a bulky man, with white hair and pale skin flushed slightly pink.

"I doubt you need fear," the Committee member said. "The latest candidate is a male Welfaro. One named Mok. Born in the slums of Old Newyork. He can't even read. Who knows what Cambridge was thinking? As I said, we have nothing to fear."

"Don't tell me what I need or need not fear," His Worldship said. Although he barely spoke above a whisper, his anger was obvious. "I have a billion dollars worth of investors ready—investors who will kill me in the blink of an eye if I lose their money. And I have a hundred million of my own dollars at stake. This candidate must fail. We *must* take Old Newyork."

The Committee member stared at the wall, too afraid to make eye contact. "Yes, your Worldship. We both know in one month the Senate will vote on your proposal to drop a heat bomb on Old Newyork. This candidate will fail, and Cambridge will have nothing to convince the Senate to vote otherwise. Then—"

"I know what will happen then, fool. That is why I've promised you a Senate post and a share of the investment. You know full well that the stakes are too high to risk any mistakes. Return to Cambridge. Watch the proceedings closely. Report as needed."

"I shall keep you informed, your Worldship," the first man said.

"Of course you will. You are too far into this to go any direction but where I order."

# CHAPTER 5

**OLD NEWYORK.** Miles and Lee hid behind a wide col-
lapsed beam, hoping the tunnel walls would not
cave in farther. Dust dotted a shaft of sunlight that
dropped into the subway tunnel through a grate.
Rats squeaked and rustled in the semi-darkness beyond the shaft of light.

Miles and Lee were not enjoying their wait.

"You want to tell me that Technocrats actually
came down here?" Lee asked. "Rode with Welfaros
in cars along those tracks?"

"They called it the subway," Miles whispered.
"They rode in the hundreds, all packed together. Before the Water Wars, fool. You know, after the dawn
of the computer age. I wish they'd teach you rookies
something about history."

Lee opened his mouth to protest, but Miles elbowed
him into silence. "In case you haven't noticed, I've
kept my voice to a whisper. And that's only to answer
your stupid questions. I'd rather not speak at all."

"Stupid questions? I—"

"Quiet," Miles elbowed Lee again. "If he hears
us, it might take us days to find him again. This guy
is fast and smart. How much longer do *you* want to
stay in Old Newyork?"

Lee wisely shut his mouth. He didn't believe Miles's story anyway. As if Technocrats would travel with Welfaros. Miles thought he knew everything, but Lee was sure that what he didn't know, he made up.

Lee just wanted back to Mainside. Real food. Real beds. And, of course, a real shower. He wanted to shower so badly he had already decided to take some of his risk pay and buy an extra five minutes of warm, wonderful water. No, make that twenty minutes. He deserved it after days in Old Newyork. And it would be a real shower. Not one of the disinfecting showers they'd face before they were allowed back Mainside. He'd sing in the shower and . . .

Miles was elbowing him again.

Footsteps approached.

Mok moved into the shaft of sunlight. It showed him for the mongrel he was. Any fool could look at him and see there'd been no clear bloodlines into his genetics since before the Water War. Here was someone with mixed ancestry as clear as the assembled features of his face. Asian eyes. Darker skin. High cheekbones. Dark, curly hair.

"Stop," Miles ordered, stepping out from behind the beam.

Lee remained hidden. It was standard field op policy. Never let the enemy understand your full force. Not that it made a difference here. Miles held the 'tric shooter chest high in both hands, training it on Mok.

Mok stopped.

"Good," Miles said. "You're making my job easy."

"Job? Are you with a work gang?"

"Nope. And before you say another word, I'm going to stun you." Miles smiled. "It's that simple."

Miles squeezed the trigger. A high-volt beam crackled from the 'tric shooter and arced the short distance into Mok's chest.

# CHAPTER 6

**MAINSIDE.** It was a large room on the tenth floor of the luxury high-rise. The Committee kept it mainly empty. That made security much easier. No one could disturb or monitor the activities on the tenth floor.

Cambridge stood near the door, waiting. At the far side of the room, the nitrogen cooling system of the super computer hummed quietly. Two comtechs stood nearby, waiting too.

Five minutes later, the elevator bells rang. Cambridge did not relax until a doctor entered, followed by three medtechs who wheeled a high narrow cot into the room. Mok's body, on top of the cot, was covered with a blanket. Cambridge knew what route the field ops had taken to bring Mok to Mainside. Seeing the covered body briefly turned Cambridge's thoughts back in time.

Nearly twenty years earlier, Cambridge had stood on the dock and watched the old man leave for Old Newyork. Only rebels, outcasts, and criminals lost themselves in Old Newyork, so the World United government never stopped anyone from going there. In fact, Old Newyork was such a convenient dumping ground, all criminals were sent there.

Getting to Old Newyork, as Cambridge had seen,

was as simple as stepping onto the next ferry. But that was the last simple thing any passenger faced. Since the World United had abandoned it to the poor, the desperate, the dying, and the criminals, there were no hospitals, no police, and no electrical power. There, among the slums, ganglords ruled like kings.

No one was ever allowed back to Mainside for any reason.

One look at a map showed how easy it was for the World United government to transform the island into a prison. The East and Hudson rivers formed the arms of a Y on both sides. At the north, the Harlem River was a channel between the other two rivers and served as a lid of the Y.

The Mainside shores of all three rivers were zoned with a wide no-cross zone dotted with explosive mines. Beyond the mines were high electric fences, and behind those deadly fences, soldiers endlessly patrolled with guard dogs. Upstream and downstream, patrol boats waited for anyone who tried to swim, drift, or boat to freedom.

None of that had changed since the night Cambridge had watched the old man go, never to return.

What had changed was Cambridge.

Inspired by the old man's faith and sacrifice, Cambridge had vowed to set up a safe passage route from Old Newyork, much like the underground railroad that had freed slaves centuries earlier.

So, armed with the almost limitless Committee funds, Cambridge found an old map that showed the site of the Lincoln Tunnel. He had purchased land close to the original entrance. The Committee had built its high-rise building within a hundred yards of the river. Millions of dollars later, they had a tunnel from the basement of the building to the old Lincoln Tunnel entrance. More millions of dollars had gone into running a six-foot plastic tube through the length of the old tunnel, coming up in a hidden entrance on the other side of the river. Now the Committee literally had a pipeline into Old Newyork.

The passage had been finished too late to bring the old man back; his reports had ended years before. But the tunnel served a purpose. It was through this passage that the Committee shipped medical supplies for relief efforts in Old Newyork. It was through this passage that field ops went back and forth at will. It was through this passage they had smuggled Mok back to Mainside.

"He is ready, sir."

It was the doctor, taking Cambridge's mind off the past. The comtechs were busy at the super computer. Cambridge gave the young doctor—short and red-headed—full attention.

"Sir, we ran the required tests on him. Despite a lifetime of poor nutrition, he has a healthy body. It should be no problem to keep him on life-support."

"Good," Cambridge said to the doctor. "And brain-wave activity?"

The doctor dropped his head, as if trying to find courage to continue.

"Yes?" Cambridge said more softly. Cambridge

was tall, almost thin. He dressed as casually as he could—soft brown sweater and blue jeans—but he knew that his hawklike appearance, the intensity in his eyes, and his reputation all served to frighten people who did not know him. Cambridge reminded himself as often as he could—indeed prayed over it as a weakness—that he needed to be more focused on others and less wrapped up in the world of his own thoughts.

"Well, . . ." the doctor nearly stammered.

Cambridge forced himself to wait. The poor man was obviously nervous—something unusual for doctors. Cambridge did not want to make it worse for him.

"It's just that his inner-core brain waves scanned extremely high, sir."

"Is that a problem?" Cambridge asked. "I thought high inner-core readings were a sign of intelligence."

"That's just it, sir. We find it hard to believe that a slum child would show this kind of intelligence."

Cambridge smiled. "It's not a surprise to me."

"Sir?"

"Nothing, doctor. Please proceed with hooking him up to the computer. For what he is about to face, we should thank God that at least he has one thing going for him."

"Yes sir."

As the doctor walked away, Cambridge let out a deep breath. Less than a month to go. Cambridge did not want to think about what would happen if this final candidate failed.

**OLD NEWYORK.** Mok screamed in his nightmare. He saw a man step out from behind a concrete beam, a man who promised to stun him. The man pointed a strange object at Mok. A crackling arc of blue light reached into Mok's chest, tearing his consciousness away in a surge of exploding pain.

Mok woke in total darkness, trembling at the vivid memory of his nightmare. It had been years since he'd cried out in his sleep. There was too much danger that the noise would give away his hiding spot. Only once had the work gangs found him. Without parents to claim him at night, he'd been a prisoner of the factory for a month before he'd escaped. Mok had vowed never to be taken again.

Mok drew deep breaths, and tried to quiet the heaving of his chest. Calm, he told himself, reach for calm. Night was never safe for those who gave away their hiding spots. He must remain silent.

Yet as awareness returned, Mok became edgier and edgier. Why did he feel so strange?

He realized he could hear an unfamiliar sound. A sighing, the way wind sometimes pushed its way through the street canyons of Old Newyork. Sighing was not the sound he fell asleep to each night. No, he fell asleep to the steady dripping of seepage from above. He strained his ears to hear water. Nothing.

Where was the plop of water drops so familiar to him over the years?

Mok shifted and almost sat bolt upright with surprise. Long habit stopped him though. The crevice he used each night as a bed was hardly bigger than himself. Once, when he was younger, another bad dream had brought him to a sitting position. He had smacked his head against the concrete directly above. Then he fell back onto the collection of rags that served as his mattress and blankets.

Only now he wasn't on his rags!

His back was on something rougher and flatter than rags. A mat, perhaps. And it seemed he was wrapped in soft cloth. He reached above and to both sides. *His groping hands could not find the walls of concrete that usually surrounded him.*

As his eyes adjusted to the darkness, Mok also noticed faint details above him, lines of lesser darkness against black. Then pinpricks of light. Stars?

*Impossible!* Mok crawled into his hiding hole every night. Without fail he piled up rocks at the low narrow entrance to keep the rats out. How could any light reach him?

The air!

It was dry. Hot. Not damp and cold.

*How could he not be where he always slept?* He tried to remember crawling into the crevice as he did at the end of the day. With a lurch of sickness, he discovered he couldn't remember. The crackling arc of blue light came back to him not as a dream, but as something that had actually happened.

Fear washed over him. Mok hated fear. It was an enemy.

"Our father who art in heaven," he whispered in slow rhythm, "hallowed be thy name."

He knew it was ridiculous to behave like the little boy who had escaped into the wonderful tales of a precious audiobook. Yet Mok continued whispering into the darkness until he finished his favorite speech given by the Galilee Man. Mok didn't know why whispering it soothed him when he felt lonely, but it always did. Maybe, Mok thought, he liked to think about having a father of his own. The place the Galilee Man called heaven sounded nice, and Mok wanted to believe such a place could some day be home.

When Mok finished his whispering, part of the fear dissolved. His confusion, though, remained.

On his back, Mok stared at the stars that appeared through the outlines above him. He stared and waited. He had no idea how much time passed, but eventually his patience was rewarded. The gray of dawn arrived to show the outline was a window carved into a limestone wall.

Only then did he rise. He was dressed in a strange white tunic that he could not remember putting on.

Mok stepped toward a large doorway in the opposite wall and to the light outside.

# CHAPTER 8

**CYBERSPACE—EGYPT.** "The sand and rocks will shred your feet. Instead of admiring the early sun, you should go back and get your sandals. You will find them beside the water jug in your room of sleep."

Mok spun around to face the unexpected voice. He saw a wizened dwarf wearing the same kind of white tunic, leaning on a cane.

The dwarf laughed. "If only you could see your face! A man would think you had no idea where you are."

The dwarf whacked Mok's leg with the cane. "Which you don't, do you? Admit it. You're lost."

Mok was glad for the whack. It gave him a place to release his anger. Anger at his confusion. How had he gotten here? Where was he?

Standing outside this strange flat building, Mok had never before felt air so dry and hot. He had never before seen sand endless in all directions. Nor a sky without buildings. Nor a wide ribbon of water. He looked up the road from the water and saw an immense pile of square stones tapering to a point high in the sky. Never had he seen such a thing.

But Mok had seen crippled, damaged, and mutated Welfaros. There were plenty of them in Old Newyork, including dwarfs. This was something he could handle.

Mok grabbed the dwarf by the shoulders, and lifted and shook him.

"Set me down," the dwarf said, keeping his grip on his cane but not striking back. "Or I won't offer you any help."

Mok stopped his shaking, but did not set the dwarf down. He spoke between clenched teeth. "Give me help or I'll choke you."

"Choke away," the dwarf said. If he was impressed with Mok's strength, it did not show. "With me gone, you'll face execution by sunset."

Mok dropped the dwarf, who promptly whacked Mok with his cane again.

"I said *set me down*," the dwarf said angrily. "Not *drop me*."

"Where am I?" Mok asked, equally angry. He refused to rub his stinging leg; the dwarf had whacked him with great enthusiasm.

"Egypt," the dwarf answered. "Thousands of years before you were born. If you had any education at all, you would recognize that as a pyramid."

"Pyramid?" echoed Mok. He decided he was still in a dream. That could be the only explanation for this. How could he be somewhere thousands of years before he was born?

Another whack from the dwarf. "Pay attention. I don't like repeating myself. What you see is a pyramid. A burial place for pharaohs."

"Pharaohs?" Mok asked.

The dwarf took another swing with his cane, but Mok was ready and grabbed it. The dwarf simply let go and grinned, leaving Mok with the short piece of wood in his hand, feeling a little silly.

"Ignorance, allow for the ignorance," the dwarf said, more to himself than to Mok. "Pharaohs are kings. Rulers of many people. They realize one great truth. No matter how rich and powerful you are, death arrives in the same way it does for the poor. These kings want a place to safeguard their bodies for eternity. They believe that as long as their bodies remain intact they will enjoy life beyond."

Mok nodded. His brain felt numb as he tried to think through this unreal situation.

"It's disgusting actually," the dwarf said. "Once the pharaoh is dead, the royal undertaker and his assistants cut open the body. They remove all the organs and brains to store in sealed clay jars. The pharaoh's body is dried out, preserved, wrapped in linen. Then it's forever hidden in a secret burial chamber deep in the great pyramid."

The dwarf shook his head to emphasize his disgust. "Stupid idea. If that were how you really lived eternally, wouldn't you want something nicer than dried leather for a body?"

Mok suddenly laughed. "I know what's happening!"

"You do?" The dwarf munched his face in puzzlement, something that, given his extensive wrinkles, was a remarkable sight.

"Glo-glo water," Mok said. "Somewhere during

the day, I must have drunk water with glo-glo pharmaceuds. Serves me right for robbing the water barons. I'll wake up in a gutter somewhere with a terrible headache. No wonder I've always refused the stuff before. And there's no way I'll touch it again. This is enough to twist my brain."

Mok snapped his fingers. "Hey, why don't I give you a name? Like . . . like Stinko. It seems to suit you."

"You can't name me." The dwarf stamped his left foot. "I already have a name. Blake."

"This is my dream. I can name you what I want."

"Blake," the dwarf insisted. "Call me anything else and I won't listen. And if it makes you feel better, go ahead and think this is a dream. Later in the day, just remember I warned you."

Mok kept laughing. "Oh really?"

"Really," the dwarf said without humor. "You see, yesterday Pharaoh Cheops died."

"So," Mok said, "even if this isn't a dream, I never knew him. What do I care?"

"You should. There's a reason you are here to inspect the pyramid. You're the royal undertaker."

# CHAPTER 9

**MOK STOOD IN THE CENTER** of a long, narrow boat, looking at the red desert hills and wide skies on both sides of him. He was leaving behind the valley of the pyramids, and leaving behind the dumb dwarf.

He stood at the prow. Behind him, a team of rowers pulled to the rhythm of a drum. A full sail on a single mast helped push the boat upstream.

Not only did he enjoy being important enough to have all these men working so hard for him, but Mok also enjoyed the sway of the water and the breeze against his face. What a nice dream. The street canyons of Old Newyork were dirty and crowded in comparison. Here irrigated fields lined both sides of the river. Tall green plants grew along its edge, three times the height of a man. The boatsman at the steering rudder had called the plants papyrus and then had frowned at Mok because of his question.

Mok didn't care. He was entertained by this dream and proud of his imagination, something he had never known could be this rich.

Stinko had told him the wide ribbon of water was the river Nile, uncontaminated water that flowed for thousands of miles. Stinko had told him the pyramid took tens of thousands of men more than ten years to build. Hundreds upon hundreds of ten-ton blocks of stone had been hauled across the desert and set on top of each other to form the pyramid. Stinko told him again it had been built for the sake of one man, someone who wanted a safe place to hide his body when he died.

*It's remarkable,* Mok thought, *that my mind was able to come up with of all of this, including a bad-tempered, smelly dwarf.* It was so ridiculous it confirmed for Mok this could only be a dream. As if clear water could flow for thousands of miles without armies fighting for it. It was so ridiculous it made him want to laugh. Perhaps when the glo-glo pharmaceuds wore off, he should become a corner storyteller, earning water instead of stealing it to give to others.

Ahead, Mok saw clusters of low, square white buildings on the west bank of the river. As the boat drew nearer, he saw clusters of the buildings stretch for a considerable distance.

"Boatsman," Mok called.

"Yes, royal undertaker." The boatsman wore a pale cotton skirt, bound in a knot at the front. Mok had kept his laughter to himself, thinking that even in a dream a man had a right to dress as he pleased.

"Tell me, does the town have a name?"

The boatsman frowned again at Mok. "Memphis, the capital. Your destination. Where the royal court lies."

"Watch your attitude," Mok growled. "I'll have you whipped."

The man bowed in instant fright.

"It was a joke," Mok said quickly. Didn't anyone in this dream have a sense of humor?

The boatsman straightened but did not dare look Mok in the face again. Mok walked to the front of the boat and thought about the work he had given himself in his dream. Royal undertaker. If the rest of his dream was as rich as this, it would be fun to find out what lay ahead.

# CHAPTER 10

**HIS NEW GUIDE** was hardly older than a girl—dark-haired, brown-eyed, and wearing a simple wrap much like Mok's. As he stepped off the boat, she waited to show him the way. Mok wanted to wander the busy streets. But she was firm in leading him to a two-wheeled vehicle attached by long, thin leather straps to large beasts.

"In the chariot, sir," she said. "We have the fastest horses possible."

Chariot. Horses. Mok made a note to remember. Yes, he would tell this story on a street corner. What a crowd of Welfaros it would draw. Of course, they wouldn't believe it either, but it might earn him a couple days' worth of water.

With a crack of the whips, the charioteer drove the horses ahead, scattering a flock of geese that a boy was herding down the road ahead of them. They quickly left behind the squawking birds and the shouting boy. Within minutes, they arrived at the temple gates.

It was an impressive building, guarded by a statue of a giant cat with a man's head. Beyond the giant columns, Mok saw a courtyard filled with dozens of wailing women.

He didn't have time to comment.

His guide stepped down from the chariot. When he joined her, she took his arm again and led him into the courtyard.

Mok watched in amazement as the women around him howled and threw dust over their heads. His guide saw his face.

"Many are professional mourners, of course," she said, as if agreeing with him. "Yet it is amazing how truly sad they are. We all deeply grieve the pharaoh's death."

He opened his mouth to ask for more explanation, but she cut him off.

"Come," she said, "your assistants await you."

She led him into the shade of a hallway at the end of the courtyard. He followed her into the depths of the temple.


There were close to two dozen men in the stone-walled room, all wearing the silly white skirts, all silent, all intent on the tables before them.

Mok put his hands on his hips and tried to make sense of the scene. Body-sized baskets. Large clay jars. Piles of white powder. A horrible smell. And—

Mok jumped back. One of the men was pushing wax up the nose of a body!

"What are you doing!" Mok could not help but blurt out his question.

The man stepped back from the table and bowed. "You have my apologies, sir. It's just that—"

Another man moved beside Mok. This one had a hooked nose and was slightly cross-eyed. "As your chief assistant, I took it upon myself to order him to begin with the beeswax. With you inspecting the temple at the pyramid, I had no idea when you might return. I did not want to delay the process."

Mok remembered what the dwarf had told him about preparing a body for the tomb. "Oh yes," Mok said. He breathed through his mouth as he spoke. *What a stench!* "I'm glad you decided not to wait for me."

Mok turned his head and rolled his eyes. This dream was hilarious.

"Continue your work," Mok said when he felt he had stifled his laughter enough to speak again. He deepened his voice for melodramatic authority. "Let's get him all wrapped up by evening."

Mok wondered if anyone in the room would chuckle. On the different tables, other bodies were in various stages of preparation. Many bodies were wrapped in linen, and Mok was pleased with his little pun.

"Sir! This is the pharaoh! Joke if you will about the common noblemen, but the pharaoh . . ."

The chief assistant clasped his hands together. His voice rose, almost in panic. "It will take hours to fill him the white natron powder. Then forty days if we want the powder to dry him properly. And after that—"

"Whatever you say." Mok was not interested in

more details. Still, he thought dreams were great. In dreams, Mok didn't have to take death so seriously. "Go ahead. Don't keep the pharaoh waiting."

"Undertaker," a voice said from the doorway.

Mok turned to see a soldier standing at the entrance. The soldier was a giant, armed with a spear and shield.

"Yes?"

"I have orders to take you to the inner chamber." The soldier pointed the spear at Mok's chest. "At once."

# CHAPTER 11

**MOK HAD NOT MINDED** when the soldier had pushed him at spearpoint to a small room hidden in the far corner of the temple. After all, Mok thought, not knowing what would happen next just added to his entertainment.

Waiting in the stillness of the small room, however, was less amusing. Especially since the soldier had refused to tell Mok anything about who he waited for.

Mok killed time by studying the strange symbols carved into the walls. There were women with six arms each. Men with dog's heads. Coiled cobras. Dancing figures. Fighting figures. Figures in boats.

He stepped forward to run his fingers over the carvings but stopped as he heard a rustling of soft cloth and the light flip-flop of sandaled footsteps. Perfume filled the air.

A woman had stepped into the chamber behind him. Without turning, Mok grinned. *Naturally,* he told himself, *if this is going to be a decent dream, somewhere along the way there should be a woman in it.* Now that he thought about it, Mok was disappointed he had taken so long to do the obvious. He should have dreamed her into sitting beside his sleeping mat. Then, as he woke, she could have been there, offering to feed him grapes, something he'd never tasted but had heard were wonderful.

He kept grinning straight ahead. Oh well, better late than never. Before turning around, he ordered himself to make her beautiful.

He finally turned.

The woman wore a long, formless dress. She was tall and slim. Her hair, shoulder length and cropped to a blunt edge, gleamed black in the sunlight provided by openings high in the chamber wall. A gold band circled her forehead. A coiling gold cobra on the band gleamed in the light from a shaft above.

And she was beautiful far beyond what he believed his imagination to be capable.

"I am Raha, daughter of the Pharaoh Cheops."

Mok would have been happy with just beautiful. But to make her wealthy and royal too? What a masterpiece of a dream.

"I am Mok," he said. Mok hoped he wouldn't wake up too soon. But, in case he was about to wake, he wanted to get to the good part right away.

"Any time now," he said, "I give you permission to declare your love for me."

She clapped her hands three times, the sound hollow and loud in the stone chamber.

"What insolence," she said. Three large men armed with spears entered the room. "All the more reason to have you arrested."

Mok laughed. "Arrested? You can't do that."

The guards rushed forward and grabbed him.

"During the night, three golden necklaces were taken from my father's body," Raha said. "As royal undertaker, you are responsible for the actions of your assistants. Accordingly, you will all be executed."

Mok grinned more. This was his world, and he could do what he wanted. He thought briefly. He decided he would defeat the guards and let her swoon over his bravery. After that, he would find the guilty assistant, accept her gratitude, and let the dream continue where it might.

He hoped all of this would last as long as possible. This was a much better world than Old Newyork and his cramped hiding hole in the damp cold tunnels below the streets.

Keeping his plan in mind, Mok slammed his heel down on a guard's toes.

He waited for the guard to hop around and look like an idiot.

Instead, the guard punched a heavy fist into Mok's face. Mok felt his head snap back and blood begin to pour from his nose. *What was wrong with this dream?*

Mok held his bleeding nose with one hand and brought his other arm back to punch the guard. The other two soldiers jabbed their spears at his face, stopping just below his chin.

He froze. Blood ran through his fingers.

"Enough," Raha said. "Take him away. No need to punish him now. He'll be dead by sunset."

**MAINSIDE.** The Committee members followed Mok's activities on the large vidscreen in the conference room. One man excused himself to use the washroom. He followed the hallway, but strode past the clearly marked washroom door.

Hidden in a stairwell, he pulled a satellite-phone from his suit pocket and flipped it open to the tiny vidscreen. He dialed a number and waited for the screen to come life.

"This better be a scrambled signal," the president's face in the vidscreen snarled as greeting. "And it better be important."

The screen was too small to show any background, and the man was smart enough not to ask what he had interrupted.

"We will not be overheard," the man answered. "I am calling about the Welfaro."

"Make it quick."

"The Welfaro is well into the first cyberstage. His body is responding well to the life-support machine. His brain wave activities show high intelligence."

"I am disturbed. As I recall from your reports," the president said, "the other candidates went into a panic as soon as they woke up in ancient Egypt."

"That is true, your Worldship. Even with training. And this one did not have any training to help him . . ."

"I am uneasy."

"Your Worldship?"

"Cambridge knows there is little time. Each of the other Committee members chose a highly educated Technocrat. When Cambridge finally had his turn, why did he choose a mere Welfaro when all the Technocrats failed?"

"Your Worldship, truly there is nothing to fear. Had you hired me earlier, during the testing of the other candidates, you would know the virtual reality of cyberspace has constraints."

"Explain."

"At the precise moment of death in cybertime, the brain monitors in real-time show total stoppage of all wave activity." The second man grinned. "Total, permanent stoppage. His brain will literally fry. If he believes he dies in cyberspace, he will die here."

"And?"

"This one is about to face a grave test, which I am sure he will fail. He faces either execution or a prison riot. None of the others found a way to avoid either."

The president smiled. "Report to me when this one is dead."

**CYBERSPACE—EGYPT.** Execution. At sunset.

Mok looked around the large underground prison. Smoky oil torches gave uncertain light. He was unable to see the expressions on the faces of his fellow prisoners. Most, like Mok, sat silently against the stone walls.

There were twenty altogether. Assistants to the royal undertaker. *His* assistants, if he were to believe the events of the day.

Mok half-expected to wake from a dream at any moment. How could he now be a royal undertaker in a faraway country thousands of years before his own birth? How could he be facing execution because one of these twenty assistants had stolen gold necklaces from the pharaoh's body?

It *must* be a dream, he told himself.

Yet, it could not be a dream. How could a Welfaro of the slums of Old Newyork have imagined this world, down to the last details of smoking, flickering oil torches? Mok touched his swelling face. It showed even more reality. The guard had punched him. Didn't one wake up from a dream instead of bleed and suffer?

He heard muttering from the other men. He looked at the far end of the prison, where the chimney of a cooking firepit was set into the wall. A tiny man stepped from the ashes.

As if he didn't face enough trouble, Mok thought, there was also the matter of this nasty little dwarf.

Blake dusted himself with great dignity, sending ashes in all directions. He marched across the prison to stand in front of Mok.

A few prisoners began to gather around the dwarf, mumbling questions.

"Leave us," Mok commanded. He was still the royal undertaker. Even in prison, he had command. The prisoners walked away.

"You can't say I didn't warn you," the dwarf said to Mok. "*Now* are you ready to ask for my help?"

"Stinko . . ." Mok began to stand.

The dwarf pushed him back down to sitting position. "Two things, you foolish puppy. One, I advise you to whisper. This will not be a conversation you'll want overheard. Do you think I crawled down that filthy chimney because I like the taste of charcoal?"

"And the second thing?" Mok managed to whisper. Sitting down, he was almost face level with the dwarf.

"My name is Blake. Not Stinko." Blake stamped his feet to make his point.

"Stinko suits you. Blake does not. Do you have any idea how ridiculous you look?" Mok remembered metal barrels of burning garbage in the street canyons of Old Newyork. Families cooked pots of food over their flames. "Your face and hands are as black as a pot's bottom."

"Insults instead of gratitude. I should turn around and climb back up that rope."

"Rope? Is it still there?"

"Put escape out of your mind. You're too large and clumsy to climb out through the chimney. Now lean forward."

Blake pulled a dagger from under his tunic. He flashed it at Mok quickly so that none of the other prisoners could see.

"Lean forward, I said!" Blake hissed. "Are you deaf? Or just stupid?"

Mok leaned forward. The dwarf stepped closer to Mok and pretended to pat his shoulders. He let the dagger fall unseen behind Mok's back.

"You are now armed," the dwarf said, stepping away. "Chose your moment carefully."

"One dagger against swords of a battalion of guards? If you think I'll do that, you're as crazy as you look."

"Fool," the dwarf said. "Not the guards. One of your assistants. Carefully chose a moment to plunge it in his chest."

"Kill one of the assistants? I don't understand."

"The pharaoh's daughter knows that one man in this prison is truly guilty. Kill one of them and blame him. Tell Raha that the man confessed and killed himself. Without him to speak his innocence, you and all the others will be freed."

"Why should she believe the story if the man is dead?"

"Because she wants to," Blake said. "She badly

wants someone to blame. If she can show the people she found the guilty man, they'll believe she can be a good ruler. In other words, she is more concerned about the appearance of justice than justice itself."

Mok thought about it. With every passing moment, the dream seemed more and more real. He wasn't sure if he wanted to find out how real an execution felt. Not with his nose so sore from the earlier punch.

"No," Mok said. "It's not right."

"You're such a child. What does justice matter against all the evils of the world? Or against your own life? Deliver her a thief—even if it isn't the real thief—and she will be grateful to you. Wealth and fame will be yours."

Mok let his mind wander to what it might be like to be rich. Even in a dream.

"No," he finally said. "I will not be part of murdering an innocent man."

"What do you care?" the dwarf asked. "What does it matter?"

Mok thought of his boyhood and the audiobook that had comforted him again and again. He thought of a man from Galilee and his teachings.

"It matters," Mok said. "I will not do this great wrong."

"For one guilty man's crime, all twenty-one of you will be executed. Yet twenty of you are innocent. What is better, one dead innocent man? Or twenty?"

"Unless by chance it happens that I stab the

guilty man, he, too, would be set free." Mok said, angry. "Should an innocent man die to save the guilty?"

The dwarf shrugged. "Do you have some way to make the thief confess? Is there a mark of guilt on him, as plain to see as this soot on my own face? No, young fool, if the thief hasn't confessed by now, don't expect him to do so by sunset. And at sunset, I remind you, you will die."

Without a backward glance, but with a grin spreading across his face, Blake the dwarf marched away from Mok. The young man from Old Newyork had passed the Committee's first test. Blake was pleased. He stepped into the firepit, jumped upward, and disappeared.

**MOK STARED THOUGHTFULLY** at the empty firepit.

He would not murder anyone. He had seen plenty of cruel deaths in Old Newyork, but he would not consider killing a man. Not even to save his own life.

He thought longer. If only there *were* some way to mark the guilty man like the soot on the dwarf's face.

*Like the soot on the dwarf's face! Black as a pot's bottom! Just like the cooking pots in Old Newyork!*

"Guard!" Mok suddenly shouted. He rose and stepped toward the door of the prison. "Guard! I wish to speak to Raha, the pharaoh's daughter!"

"There is the rooster you requested," Raha said, pointing at a servant who held the squawking bird upside down by its feet. "And a well-used cooking pot. Remember our agreement. If this fails, *you* shall be executed instead of the guilty man."

Mok remembered. It was the only way he'd been able to convince Raha to agree. Of course, what did it matter to him if they were all to be executed anyway?

"Anything else?" she asked. They were standing just outside of the prison door.

"After I go back into the prison cell, you will remain here," Mok reminded her. "When I call for it, send the guards in with torches."

"That sounds close to an order," she said. "Must I have you again punished?"

She was unable to hide her smile completely. Was she proud of Mok and his idea? Mok began to really hope this wasn't a dream. If this worked, perhaps he could spend more time with the pharaoh's daughter. Beautiful, wealthy, royal . . .

"Enough wasting of time." She clapped her hands. "Guards, open the prison door."

Mok took the feet of the flapping rooster in one hand, the handle of the cooking pot in the other. He stepped back inside the prison.

All twenty of his assistants stared at him in puzzlement.

Mok waited until the prison door shut behind him.

"There is a custom to determine a man's guilt," Mok began with as much authority as he could force into his voice. "Not once has this custom failed."

He had their full attention.

Mok lifted the rooster higher. He shook it until it squawked with rage.

"This is the sound of guilt," Mok said.

The assistants began to speak among themselves.

"Yes," Mok said, silencing them. He moved to the center of the room. In full view of all the prisoners, he overturned the pot. With quick movements, he stuffed the rooster beneath the upside-down pot. It stopped squawking immediately.

"And this silence," Mok said, pointing at the now quiet pot, "is the sound of innocence."

He looked at all the men. "You see, a rooster covered in complete darkness knows the presence of a guilty man."

He let them speak for a few moments, then lifted his hand for silence.

"*Complete* darkness," Mok said. "We will form a line. The torches will be extinguished. One by one, each will step past this pot. One by one, each will place his hands squarely on the bottom of this pot and press hard. When the guilty man touches the pot, the rooster beneath it will crow. The guilty man shall take his punishment. The rest of us will live."

Mok let them speak as he moved along the prison walls. One by one he lifted the torches and stubbed out their flames on the hard ground. When he held the final torch, he turned to the men.

The prisoners had formed their line before the overturned pot. Mok extinguished the torch and the room became totally dark.

"Begin," Mok commanded.

Slow shuffling in the darkness filled the silence.

Mok wondered if they could hear his heart pound out its fear. Surely the rooster would help him find the guilty man . . .

The rooster did not crow. The last of the prisoners touched the pot and called out to Mok.

"Guard!" Mok shouted. This was the moment. If his plan had worked, he would live. If not . . .

# CHAPTER 15

**NOT ONE, BUT FIVE GUARDS** immediately entered the prison. Their torches gave new light and new shadows.

Raha followed them. She stopped and folded her arms.

"Form a line," Raha commanded the prisoners. "Walk past me and show me the palms of your hands."

Mok stood close to her. He, too, wanted to see the palms of each prisoner's hands.

The first prisoner showed palms covered with black smudges—as sooty as the dwarf's hands and face had been. Each of the next ten prisoners also showed soot from the pot's bottom, a result of its years over cooking fires.

Then came the eleventh prisoner, the chief assistant. He showed no fear. But when he showed his palms, they were clean.

Raha nodded, and the guards descended on the man, holding his arms as Raha faced him.

"Where are the necklaces?" Raha demanded.

"Your highness?" The chief assistant sagged in fear. The guards held him upright. "I do not understand. Why accuse me?"

"Because your palms are clean," she said. "Why

did you not touch the pot? Did you fear the rooster might actually crow and declare your guilt? Instead, you have declared it upon yourself."

The man looked stunned.

"Take him away," she told the guards. "If he tells us where to find the necklaces, his death will be fast and merciful."

She turned to Mok, no longer hiding the smile on her face. "As for you," she said, "you will dine with me."

She stepped toward him and offered the back of her hand.

Mok took it, amazed at the softness of her skin. He lifted it to his mouth, and kissed it. Perfume filled his nostrils. He kissed it again and lifted his eyes to hers.

"Raha," he began.

But he was not able to finish. The room suddenly turned black. It began spinning. Spinning. Spinning . . .

# CHAPTER 16

**MAINSIDE.** There was only one Committee member who did not take joy in the news that Mok had become the first candidate to move to the next cyberspace test.

This Committee member secretly hurried to a netphone in the main floor lobby of the building. Unless someone was there to look over his shoulder as he typed, this was the safest and fastest way to send a message.

When the lobby was empty, the Committee member hit the private dotcom number of the president of the World United. When the system prompted him for his e-mail message, the Committee member typed in a few hurried sentences:

> Warning. Candidate has passed first test. Nothing to fear. Failure at next stage is certain. Will confirm this with face-to-face vidconference at first opportunity.

The Committee member checked over his message. He was satisfied it said enough . . . for now.

He hit the send button on the netphone keypad.

## CHAPTER 17

**CYBERSPACE—THE HOLY LAND (A.D. 1296).** Night. Stars above. A breeze on his face. Hundreds of small scattered fires flickered below.

*Raha?* Mok wondered. Where was Raha? Where was the linen tunic he had worn?

His clothes were rough, heavy. He seemed to be standing on the edge of a great building. What madness was this?

"I see you've come to join us. Pray tell, how did you escape execution?"

"Stinko!" Mok was almost glad for a familiar voice.

The dwarf's cane whacked at him from the darkness.

"How many times must I tell you not to call me that—"

"Where am I?" Mok said. "Why do you follow me?"

The dwarf sighed. "We are on the ramparts of a castle. In the Holy Land of Jesus Christ. You are part of a great crusade in his name and—"

"Blake!" Mok was so excited he forgot to insult the dwarf. "Did you say Jesus Christ?"

"Yes . . ." The dwarf's voice was puzzled.

"That's the Galilee Man! From the audiobook I had as a boy!"

"The Galilee Man . . . I suppose a person could call him that. He did come from that region."

"Let the little children come to me," Mok recited from memory. "You see? He loved children. He made promises I've always wanted to believe. Can I find him and speak to him?"

For the first time Mok could recall, the dwarf spoke gently.

"He died more than a thousand years before this castle was built," Blake said. "You will not find him walking this land."

The dwarf paused. "Sleep now. Tomorrow, daylight will show you those fires belong to a great army surrounding this castle. You are in the middle of a siege. It will not end until every man, woman, and child within the castle walls has died. Including you."

# AUTHOR NOTE

Mok's story is actually two stories. One of the stories, of course, is described in this cyberepisode.

There is also a series story linking together all the CyberQuest books—the reason Mok has been sent into cyberspace. That story starts in Pharaoh's Tomb (#1) and is completed in Galilee Man (#6). No matter where you start reading Mok's story, you can easily go back to any book in the series without feeling like you already know too much about how the series story will end.

This series story takes place about a hundred years in the future. You will see that parts of Mok's world are dark and grim. Yet, in the end, this is a story of hope, the most important hope any of us can have. We, too, live in a world that at times can be dark and grim. During his cyberquest, Mok will see how Jesus Christ and his followers have made a difference over the ages.

Some of you may be reading these books after following Mok's adventures in Breakaway, a Focus on the Family magazine for teen guys. Those magazine episodes were the inspiration for the CyberQuest series, and I would like to thank Michael Ross and Jesse Flores at Breakaway for *all the fun we had working together. However, this series contains far more than the original stories—once I really started to explore Mok's world, it became obvious to me that there was too much of the story left to be told. So, if you're joining this adventure because of* Breakaway, *I think I can still promise you plenty of surprises.*

*Last, thank you for sharing Mok's world with me. You are the ones who truly bring Mok and his friends and enemies to life.*

From your friend,

Sigmund Brouwer

*The adventure continues!*

Join Mok in an ancient castle in

## QUEST 2

## KNIGHT'S HONOR

The great castle overlooks the hills of the
Holy Land. Now, in the year of Our Lord 1296,
the walls are about to fall to a savage army.
Mok has been thrust into the battle, with only
days to live. He can save those around him,
but only if he betrays his soul. And behind
it all, there remains his quest for the
truth about the Galilee Man.